Good for You, Good for Me

English edition first published in Australia and New Zealand in 2009 by Gecko Press
PO Box 9335, Marion Square, Wellington 6141, New Zealand
info@geckopress.com

Original title: Ich mit dir, du mit mir
Copyright © 2008 Atlantis, an imprint of Orell Füssli Verlag AG, Zürich, Switzerland
All rights reserved.

English translation © Gecko Press 2009

National Library of New Zealand Cataloguing-in-Publication Data

Pauli, Lorenz.
Ich mit dir, du mit mir. English
Good for you, good for me / Lorenz Pauli, Kathrin Schärer.
ISBN 978-1-87746-739-4 (hbk.) — 978-1-87746-738-7 (pbk.)
[1. Bears—Fiction. 2. Dormice—Fiction. 3. Games—Fiction.
4. Friendship—Fiction.] I. Schärer, Kathrin. II. Title.
833.92—dc 22

Translated by Catherine Chidgey
Edited by Penelope Todd
Typesetting: Vida & Luke Kelly, Wellington, New Zealand
Printing: Everbest, China

ISBN paperback 978-1-877467-38-7
ISBN hardback 978-1-877467-39-4

For more curiously good books, please visit www.geckopress.com

Good for You, Good for Me

Written by **Lorenz Pauli**, illustrated by **Kathrin Schärer**

GECKO PRESS

In the distance, there was music. Bear was sitting out on his favourite red cushion.
He pricked up his ears. The music made him feel happy.

Then along came Dormouse with his flute.

'Dormouse, I'd like to try that,' said Bear. 'Shall we swap?
I could give you my cushion for your flute.
Then you can rest after all your walking, and I'll play you some tunes.
That's good for you, good for me.'

Dormouse agreed and lay down on the still-warm cushion.

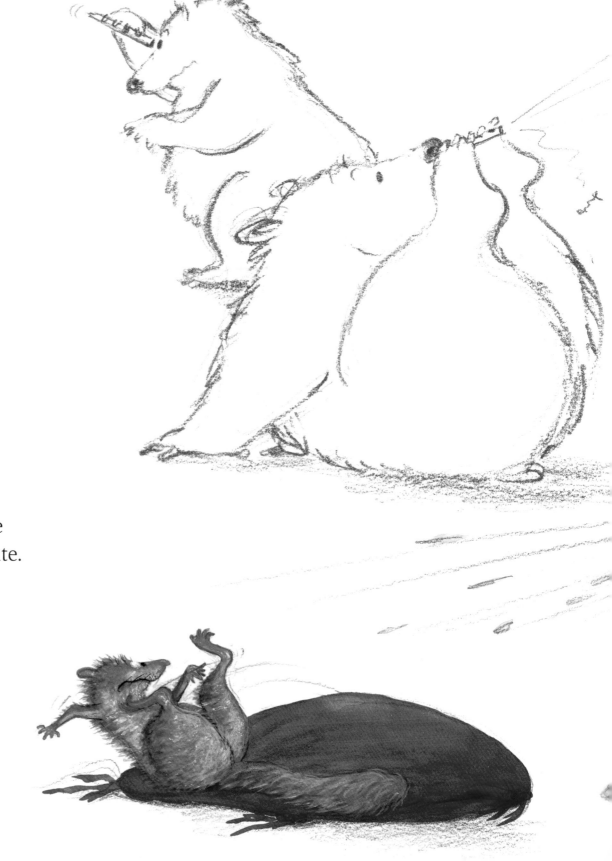

Bear blew hard.

His great big claws and furry paws were
too big for the holes in the tiny little flute.

But bears don't give up easily.

He tried with his front paws.
He tried with his back paws.

He huffed and he puffed.

'Stop that screeching!' Dormouse shrieked.
'I need peace and quiet to rest.'

Bear was bamboozled. What use is a flute
if you can't tootle on it?

Dormouse had a suggestion: 'If I play the flute, we'll have music.
Shall we swap? You give me your flute and I'll give you music.
Good for you, good for me.'

Bear scratched his ear. Whose flute for whose music? Was this a good swap?

Finally he nodded and gave the flute to Dormouse.
Bear sat on the ground and listened. Dormouse played rather well
sitting on Bear's cushion.

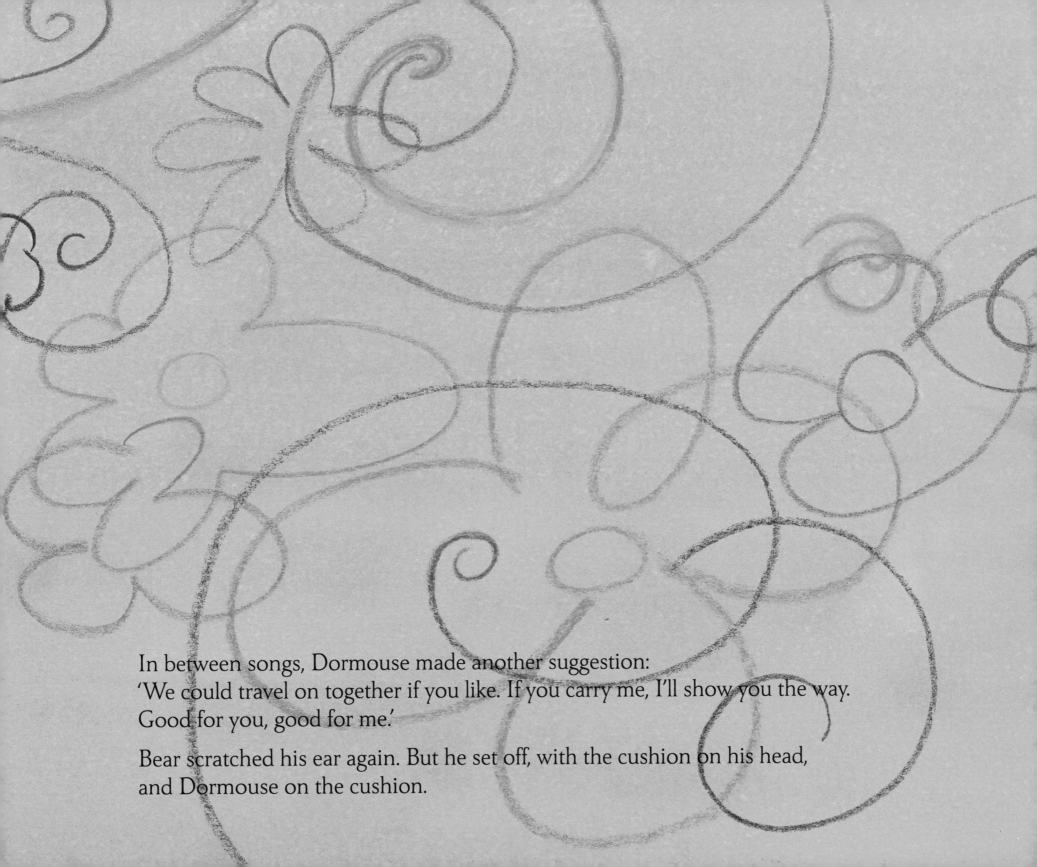

In between songs, Dormouse made another suggestion:
'We could travel on together if you like. If you carry me, I'll show you the way.
Good for you, good for me.'

Bear scratched his ear again. But he set off, with the cushion on his head,
and Dormouse on the cushion.

Up on the hill, beneath the oak tree, they stopped for a rest —
Bear on the soft grass, Dormouse on the soft fur,
and the flute on the soft cushion.

Dormouse woke Bear by playing the flute.

Bear shook his paws; he snapped his claws and clucked his tongue.
He wiggled his ears and waggled his bottom. He drummed
on his tum, he hopped, he skipped, he danced.

And danced!

And danced!!

Bear was dizzy, dizzy with joy.
He flopped on the grass.

'Don't stop – keep dancing, Bear!'
said Dormouse. 'I can't dance,
but watching you, I feel light as a feather.
Dance for me, and I'll give you a
lucky pebble...
Good for you, good for me.'

Bear danced for Dormouse. He danced with Dormouse.
They laughed and danced until they fell over.

But now dusk was falling. It was time to go back to the forest.
Dormouse skipped along with the flute and Bear followed, dancing.
Happily, Bear threw his lucky pebble high and caught it again.

But then the pebble fell into a hazelnut bush.

Bear shook the branches and a couple of nuts fell.
Dormouse was overjoyed: 'Rattle and shake till all
the nuts are down! If you help me gather them,
I'll give you this pretty pebble. It fell from the sky
just this minute. Good for you, good for me.'

Bear scratched behind his ear.
Isn't that the same pebble he just...?

But he shook the hazelnut bush
with all his might.

Little by little, it grew dark –
too dark to collect nuts.

Dormouse gave Bear
the pebble.

Bear looked at the pebble and thought about all the things
he and Dormouse had swapped.

He wondered: What do I want with a cushion? All I need is my warm, soft fur.
Do I really need a flute when I can whistle my songs instead?
And what about this lucky pebble? Luck seems to find me anyway.

Bear said softly, 'Here, my friend, you can have my lucky pebble.
That would make me happy. Good for you, good for me.'

Dormouse was astounded.

Then he snuggled up to Bear and said,
'Yes, giving does feel wonderful...
Say, I'll give you the moonlight on the water.'

Bear was delighted. 'And I'll give you
the scent of the flowers.'

'And I'll give you the sigh of the wind.'

'And tomorrow, at sunrise, when all the colours
are coming alive, we'll give each other the reds...
and the greens! The yellows! And the blues!'
said Bear.

'What if it's raining?'

'Raining? Hmm, let's wait and see...'